Hanna Meets A Mud Wump

by
Jody Burmeister

Illustrated by Joyce Steffens Dunseth

Library of Congress Catalog Card Number: 96–71183

Publisher's Cataloging in Publication
(Prepared by Quality Books, Inc.)

Burmeister, Jody.
    Hanna Meets a Mud Wump / Jody Burmeister.
    p.cm.
    SUMMARY: Hanna, a Doberman puppy, makes friends with a Mud Wump, a creature living in mud who is in need of help.
    ISBN: 1–882791–37–8

    I. Title.
PZ7.B8754Mu 1997   [E]
                    QBI96–40714

Proctor Publications, LLC

P.O. Box 2498, Ann Arbor, Michigan, 48106 • (800) 343–3034

First Edition
Printed in Singapore

Dedicated to our children,
grandchildren,
family and friends.

•

With thanks to Julayne Hughes
for editing
and encouragement.

Birthplace
of the
Mud Wump

BIRTH OF THE MUD WUMP

One night, during a deep sleep, an adorable little critter appeared in a very realistic dream. When morning came, the Mud Wump name came to mind. When looking in reference books verified no such critter existed, apprehension quickly turned into happiness as I realized the Mud Wump would soon become a reality. He had already been created in my subconscious, and would shortly be born onto a sketch pad.

Now this lovable little Mud Wump can enter the hearts of boys and girls, moms and dads, grandmas and grandpas everywhere, inviting the child in all of us to feel loved and needed by a Mud Wump!

We would like to introduce you to Hanna and the Mud Wump, a delightful pair of fictional characters that will thrill children of all ages. The Hanna and the Mud Wump series was developed combining an invented underground creature called the Mud Wump and a lovable, if somewhat klutzy, Doberman puppy named Hanna. Both came from families who cared about their youngsters much the same as people do.

When Hanna and the Mud Wump are together, all sorts of everyday problems come to the surface and are wisely handled by Hanna. Consequently, their adventures can be used as a positive learning experience for boys and girls. Each rhyming story has a different topic and was written to bring the concerns of children out in the open. We believe this approach will instill self-confidence and a feeling of well being in even the most sensitive child.

Until a young Mud Wump

ventured out of his home

one winter day,

All Mud Wumps had remained

in the earth under their

sturdy roofs of clay.

This little Mud Wump

left the safety

of his puddled place.

Getting into trouble

was easy for him,

with mischief written

all over his face.

When he disobeyed his parents,

he got caught like a fish.

He got stuck this time

in a stack of newspapers,

he could feel himself squish.

Then he remembered hearing,

"Come, Hanna, come,"

from his home beneath the yard.

Hanna might be the perfect one

to ask for help,

becoming friends

shouldn't be too hard.

Hanna was a Doberman pup,

gentle as a baby lamb or doe.

Children fell in love

with her playful ways,

wherever she would go.

She wasn't very brave at all,

from her own shadow

she would flee.

Sometimes when she got really scared,

she would hide behind a tree.

Hanna was playing in her yard

when she heard

"Help me!"

A tiny voice seemed to be

coming from under the tree.

Hanna's curiosity made her drop

her twig and sniff all around

to find this critter.

Then she found

a mysterious creature

in the papers,

and her heart began to flitter.

She thought, "What could it be?

Oh, what could it be?

What is this creature

that has been screaming,

'Help me!'"

"I'm a Mud Wump!

And it's plain to see,

You have never encountered

anything like me!"

"I need to get back

to my mud-filled home.

Mom will be worried

because I'm not allowed

to roam!"

"So pick me up carefully,

but don't let me get warm.

When I get hot,

my whole body will transform!"

Hanna said,

"I've picked up stones

and bark from a stump,

But I have never ever picked up

a Mud Wump!"

The Mud Wump remarked,

"It will be a new experience

for both of us, it's true.

At no time have I ever

been carried by a dog

like you."

Hanna howled "Yuk!

I can't believe

what you're putting me through.

How we'll get you home now,

I haven't a single clue!"

Hanna picked up the Mud Wump

nervously, in an uneasy way.

Then her passenger started to melt,

to Hanna's dismay!

The Mud Wump cried,

"Spit me out!

I'm starting to droop!

If you're not careful,

I'll turn into a puddle of goop."

The Mud Wump despaired,

"You must think of something

and do it real fast.

If I have to stay here much longer,

I don't think I'll last!"

Hanna thought,

then got a bright idea.

"I'll eat snow!

That will help cool my mouth

down to a frigid zero!"

Then Hanna couldn't believe

what she saw with her eyes.

When the Mud Wump cooled down,

he quickly regained his size.

Then Hanna gave examples

of a fish

out of water.

How the poor little swimmer

would flitter and flutter.

"And when it rains and pours,

an earthworm squirms.

Up from the ground

come the wiggly, squiggly worms!"

"Ducks in the desert

could not find

a place to swim.

So they live

near the water

where they can

splash on a whim."

"Just like pets

need a safe and loving home,

They would find dangers

if they're allowed to roam.

"Humans, too,

need shelter

from the heat and the cold.

Their children are special,

and need to do

as they're told.

The Mud Wump said,

"Now I see

what you're trying to say.

It's never easy to survive

when you go astray."

The Mud Wump climbed into

Hanna's chilled mouth with glee.

"Being home where I belong

will be better than roaming free."

So Hanna took the Mud Wump

back to his puddled place.

The thought of leaving her newfound friend

brought tears to her face.

But they could both look forward

to good times at play.

And remember the lessons

they learned today.

Now. . . .

Come along

and we will see,

The lessons learned

for you and me.

Hanna learned

to be gentle and kind

to her new

Mud Wump friend.

Finding differences

in each other

was fun,

could even start a trend.

911

Hanna learned that by using her head,

she saved a life

and a mother Mud Wump's son.

Just like all boys and girls

can remember when they see danger

to call Nine-One-One.

The Mud Wump learned

to always listen to his parents

and never run away.

When he failed to listen,

being lost and frightened

was the price he had to pay.

He learned that you should always be careful

who you ask for help.

But aid can come from unlikely places

when you call out with a yelp.

The greatest lesson of all

was to love and respect

everything that lives.

If you don't stray from home,

you'll discover

the happiness it gives.

The lessons they learned

by being kind to each other

We can take with us through life,

whether sister or brother.

Hanna Meets a Mud Wump Series:

When the creation of the Mud Wump character was complete in her mind, Jody Burmeister realized that this lovable creature could be used in story books to help children solve many problems that aren't dealt with to a large extent in children's literature today. The Mud Wump character allows these issues to be discussed at a level children can comprehend, and gives them easy-to-understand solutions to difficult problems such as getting lost, divorce, physical challenges, and other such predicaments. Future "Hanna and the Mud Wump" books will include these and other problems children face.

ABOUT THE AUTHOR

Jody Burmeister is an author, poet, and artist. She grew up in southern Indiana, and now lives in southeastern Michigan with her husband, Bud, and her Louisiana Catahoula Leopard dog named Bayou. Hanna the Doberman, who is no longer a pup, lives happily with the author's daughter in northern California.

Jody is completing a book of poetry which entails life's happenings, giving hope and encouragement to overcome the many adversities which we are confronted with as adults. This common thread has led to the "Hanna and the Mud Wump" Tales for children, thus allowing the Adult and Child in Jody to explore life's conflicts while giving the gift of hope.

ABOUT THE ARTIST

Joyce Steffens Dunseth was born in Mount Clemens, Michigan and raised in the neighboring village of Fraser. Joyce, who earned her bachelor's degree in education and fine arts from Michigan State University, has spent much of her time teaching elementary and preschool children.

Joyce paints landscapes, waterscapes, and her own creation called Mystical Wildlife Images, which have won awards in juried shows. She has also written and illustrated her own book, "Teddy Bear Dreams."